The Coffee House of Surat

A Parable of Faith, Tolerance,
and the Search for Truth

A Modern Translation

Adapted for the Contemporary Reader

Leo Tolstoy

Translated by Tim Zengerink

Table of Contents

Preface - Message to the Reader

What If You Could Help Rebuild the Greatest Library in Human History?

Thousands of years ago, the Library of Alexandria stood as the crown jewel of human achievement — a sanctuary where the collected wisdom of every known civilization was gathered, preserved, and shared freely.

And then, it was lost.

Through fire, conquest, and the slow erosion of time, humanity lost not just books — but ideas, dreams, discoveries, and stories that could have changed the world forever.

Today, the Library of Alexandria lives again — and you are invited to be a part of its restoration.

Our mission is simple yet profound:

To rebuild the greatest library the world has ever known, and to translate all timeless works into every language and dialect, so that no seeker of knowledge is ever left behind again.

By joining our movement to rebuild the modern Library of Alexandria, you become part of an unprecedented mission:

- **Unlimited Access to the Greatest Audiobooks & eBooks Ever Written:**

  Instantly explore thousands of legendary works—Plato, Shakespeare, Jane Austen, Leo Tolstoy, and countless more. All instantly available to read or listen, placing a complete literary universe at your fingertips.

- **Beautiful Paperback & Deluxe Editions at Printing Cost**

  Own any title as an elegant paperback, deluxe hardcover, or stunning collectible boxset—offered to you at true printing cost, delivered straight to your door. Build your personal Library of Alexandria, crafted for beauty, built for durability, and worthy of proud display.

- **Fresh Translations for Modern Readers—in Every Language & Dialect**

  Enjoy timeless masterpieces reimagined in clear, contemporary language—no more outdated phrases or obscure references. Alongside the original versions, we're tirelessly translating these classics into every language and dialect imaginable, ensuring accessibility and understanding across cultures and generations.

- **Join a Global Renaissance of Literature & Knowledge**

  You directly support expanding our library, publishing deluxe editions at true cost, translating works into all global languages, and bringing humanity's greatest stories to people everywhere. By joining today, you're not just preserving a legacy of masterpieces; you set in motion a powerful wave of literary accessibility.

Become a Torchbearer of Knowledge.

Join us for free now at **LibraryofAlexandria.com**

Together, we will ensure that the light of human wisdom never fades again.

With gratitude and a shared love of knowledge,

The Modern Library of Alexandria Team

Visit:

www.libraryofalexandria.com

Or scan the code below:

Introduction

A Universal Parable of Religion, Reason, and Humility

Leo Tolstoy's The Coffee-House of Surat is a deceptively simple yet profoundly resonant parable that captures the heart of one of the most pressing spiritual questions of all time: Can one religion claim exclusive access to truth? Set in a modest coffee-house in the Indian town of Surat, this short tale brings together men of different religious traditions—a Hindu, a Muslim, a Jew, a Catholic, and a Protestant—who each insist that their own path is the only valid one. As their debate escalates, they fail to notice the quiet wisdom of a sixth figure: a Chinese man who listens attentively, says little, and finally offers a perspective that transcends dogma and division.

First published in 1893, this story is one of the clearest expressions of Tolstoy's late-life commitment to religious pluralism, ethical universality, and spiritual humility. Inspired by his reading of Eastern philosophies, especially Indian and Chinese traditions, The Coffee-House of Surat presents a vision of truth that is not confined to scripture, denomination, or theological system. Instead, it suggests that true religion resides in right action, in the pursuit of love, justice, and humility—regardless of creed.

Though the story spans only a few pages, it serves as a concise statement of Tolstoy's mature theology, which had by that time rejected the dogmatic authority of the Russian Orthodox Church in favor of a personal, rational, and morally centered form of faith. This was the same ethical Christianity that led Tolstoy to embrace nonviolence, vegetarianism, simple living, and pacifism. He admired the teachings of Jesus, particularly the Sermon on the Mount, but he saw parallels in other spiritual traditions as well. To Tolstoy, religious truth was not a property to be owned, but a light to be lived by.

In The Coffee-House of Surat, that light is obscured by pride. Each religious man speaks eloquently, quoting texts and recounting arguments, but all are driven by a desire to win, not to understand. Their failure lies not in their beliefs, but in their certainty—in their refusal to see that others, too, may know the divine. It is the Chinese man, a figure of contemplative detachment, who breaks this impasse. He tells a parable about a light seen through different windows—reminding the others that their arguments, however passionate, are limited by perspective.

The story's brevity gives it the quality of a koan or a spiritual fable. It is less about theology than about spiritual posture. It invites readers not to choose between religions, but to examine the deeper unity beneath religious differences. Its message is as timely now as it was in the 19th century: in an age marked by polarization, interfaith conflict, and ideological absolutism, Tolstoy offers a path of humility, dialogue, and shared ethical striving.

Faith Beyond Boundaries: Tolstoy's Spiritual Vision for Humanity

By the time he wrote The Coffee-House of Surat, Tolstoy had undergone a dramatic spiritual transformation. In the aftermath of personal crisis and disillusionment with institutional religion, he developed a philosophy grounded in moral action and inner sincerity rather than outward ritual or ecclesiastical authority. This shift is reflected in the Chinese man's role in the story. He is not tied to a specific creed, nor does he argue. He listens. He reflects. He speaks with gentleness and clarity. He becomes, in effect, Tolstoy's mouthpiece for a higher religious consciousness—one that is universal, practical, and rooted in the common human capacity for goodness.

The story also exemplifies Tolstoy's deepening interest in Eastern thought. He was deeply influenced by Laozi, Confucius, and Indian spiritual writings such as the Bhagavad Gita. The Chinese man in the story may be seen as an embodiment of these values: stillness, detachment, respect for the ineffable. In his presence, the clamor of doctrinal argument is silenced, not through force or counterargument, but through a simple, wise metaphor that dissolves the illusion of separateness.

And yet, The Coffee-House of Surat is not a call for relativism. Tolstoy does not argue that all ideas are equally true. Rather, he suggests that all traditions contain glimpses of the truth—and that those glimpses can be obscured by pride, tribalism, and institutional arrogance. What matters is not which flag one waves, but how one lives. A man of any religion who practices kindness, patience, humility, and justice is closer to God than a man who quotes scripture and condemns others.

Tolstoy's message, though gentle in tone, is revolutionary in implication. It calls for a new kind of religious engagement—one not rooted in conquest or conversion, but in mutual recognition and ethical

The Coffee House of Surat

(After Bernardin de Saint-Pierre)

In the town of Surat, India, there was a coffeehouse where people from different countries and backgrounds came together to share stories and have conversations.

One day, a well-known Persian scholar visited this coffeehouse. He had spent his entire life studying God, writing books, and debating religious ideas. He had thought so much about the subject that he eventually confused himself and stopped believing in God altogether. When the Shah found out, he banished the man from Persia.

After years of questioning the existence of a higher power, the scholar became so lost in his own thoughts that instead of realizing he had confused himself, he convinced himself that no greater wisdom controlled the universe.

The scholar had an African servant who always stayed by his side. When the scholar went into the coffeehouse, the servant remained outside, sitting on a stone under the scorching sun, waving away the flies.

Inside, the Persian sat comfortably on a couch and ordered a cup of opium. After drinking it, his thoughts started racing. He looked toward the open door and called out to his servant.

"Tell me, ignorant servant," he said. "Do you believe that God exists or not?"

"Of course, there is," the slave answered without hesitation. He reached under his belt and pulled out a small wooden idol.

"This," he said proudly, "is the god who has protected me since I was born. In my country, we all worship the sacred tree from which this god was carved."

The people in the coffeehouse listened to their conversation with surprise. They were shocked by the scholar's question, but even more by the slave's answer.

One of them, a Brahmin, turned to the slave and said, "You poor fool! Do you really believe that God can fit under a man's belt? There is only one true God— Brahma. He is greater than the entire world because He created it. Brahma is the supreme God, and the grand temples along the Ganges River were built in His honor. Only His true priests, the Brahmins, understand Him. Thousands of years have passed, and despite all the changes in the world, our priests have remained powerful because Brahma protects them."

The Brahmin spoke as if he had proven his point, but a Jewish merchant sitting nearby disagreed.

"No! The true house of God is not in India, and Brahma does not watch over the Brahmins. The one true God is the God of Abraham, Isaac, and Jacob. He has chosen only one people—Israel. Since the beginning of time, He has loved and protected us. If we are spread across different countries today, it is only a test of our faith. God has promised that one day He will bring us back to Jerusalem. There, our great Temple will be rebuilt, and Israel will once again be a powerful nation."

The Jewish man spoke with deep emotion, his eyes filling with tears. He wanted to continue, but before he could, an Italian missionary sitting nearby interrupted him.

"What you are saying is not true," the Italian missionary told the Jewish man. "You are making God sound unfair. He does not favor one nation over others. Even if He once blessed the Israelites, that was long ago. Nineteen hundred years have passed since they angered Him, and because of that, their nation was destroyed, and they were scattered across the world. Their religion no longer spreads, and few follow it. God does not choose one people above the rest. Instead, He welcomes all who seek salvation into the Catholic Church of Rome. Outside of it, no one can be saved."

As soon as the Italian finished speaking, a Protestant minister nearby grew pale and turned to him.

"How can you claim that salvation belongs only to your church?" he argued. "The only people who will be saved are those who worship God in spirit and truth, just as Christ commanded in the Gospel."

A Turkish official from the customs house in Surat sat in the coffeehouse, quietly smoking his pipe. Hearing the argument, he smirked and turned toward both Christian men.

"Your belief in the Roman Church is useless," he said. "Twelve hundred years ago, the true faith of Muhammad replaced it. You can see for yourselves how Islam continues to grow, spreading across Europe, Asia, and even China. You already agree that God rejected the Jews, and you claim that their religion is false because they are scattered and powerless. But look at Islam! It is strong and growing everywhere. That is proof that it is the one true faith. Only the followers of Muhammad will be saved—but not all of them, only those who follow Omar. The followers of Ali have twisted the true religion."

A Persian scholar, who followed the teachings of Ali, was about to speak. But by then, the entire coffeehouse had turned into a noisy argument. People from different religions and backgrounds debated about God and the right way to worship Him. Abyssinian Christians, Tibetan monks, Ismailis, and fire-worshippers all joined in. Each one insisted that only in their own country was the true God understood and worshipped correctly.

Everyone was arguing except for a Chinese scholar, a follower of Confucius. He sat in the corner, calmly sipping his tea and listening to the heated discussion without saying a word.

The Turk noticed the quiet man and turned to him.

"You must agree with me, my Chinese friend," he said. "You have been silent, but I know you support my argument. The traders from your country tell me that while many religions have been introduced to China, your people consider Islam the best and accept it willingly. Tell us your thoughts on the true God and His prophet."

"Yes, tell us what you believe," the others added, turning to the scholar.

The Chinese man closed his eyes for a moment, thinking. Then he slowly opened them, placed his hands inside the wide sleeves of his robe, and folded them over his chest. Speaking in a calm and steady voice, he said:

"My friends, I believe that pride is what keeps people from agreeing on matters of faith. If you are willing to listen, I will share a story that might help explain this."

"I traveled here from China on an English steamer that had sailed around the world. One day, we stopped to collect fresh water and landed on the eastern coast of Sumatra. It was noon, and some of us stepped onto the shore to rest under the shade of coconut trees near a small village. Our group included men from different countries and backgrounds.

As we sat there, a blind man approached us. Later, we learned that he had lost his sight because he had spent years staring at the sun, trying to understand what it was and how it gave light.

He had thought about it endlessly, staring directly at the sun for too long. But instead of discovering the truth, he damaged his eyes and became blind.

Then he told himself, 'The sun's light is not a liquid, because if it were, we could pour it from one container to another, and the wind would move it like water. It is not fire, because fire can be put out with water. It is not a spirit, because we can see it with our eyes. And it is not a solid object, because it cannot be touched or moved. So, since it is neither liquid, fire, spirit, nor matter, that must mean the sun does not exist at all.'

This was how he reasoned, and after staring at the sun and thinking about it so much, he lost not only his sight but also his sense of reason. And when he could no longer see, he became completely convinced that the sun did not exist.

With the blind man was his servant, who helped guide him. After settling his master in the shade, the servant picked up a fallen coconut and began making a small lamp. He twisted a wick from coconut fibers, pressed oil from the nut into the shell, and soaked the wick in it.

As the servant continued his work, the blind man sighed and said, "Well, servant, wasn't I right? I told you there is no sun, and now you sit here in darkness. People say the sun exists, but if that's true, then what is it?"

The servant answered calmly, "I don't know what the sun is, and it's not for me to question. But I do know what light is. I have made a small lamp, and with it, I can see well enough to help you and find what I need inside our hut."

Lifting the coconut shell, the servant said, "This is my sun."

A man with crutches sitting nearby heard the conversation and laughed.

"You must have been blind your entire life," the man said to the blind man. "That's the only reason you don't know what the sun is. Let me explain—it's a ball of fire that rises from the sea every morning and sets behind the mountains of our island every evening. We all see this happen every day. If you could see, you would know it too."

A fisherman who had been listening shook his head. "It's obvious you have never left this island," he said. "If you weren't crippled and had sailed the ocean like I have, you would know that the sun doesn't set behind the mountains. Just as it rises from the ocean each morning, it also sinks back into the sea every night. I watch it happen with my own eyes, so I know this is the truth."

Then an Indian man in the group joined the conversation.

"I can't believe an adult would say something so ridiculous," he said. "How could a ball of fire fall into the water without being put out? The sun is not fire at all—it is the god Deva, who rides a chariot around the golden mountain, Meru. Sometimes, evil serpents named Ragu and Ketu attack and swallow him, causing darkness on Earth. But when our priests pray, the god is set free, and the light returns. Only people who have never traveled beyond their small islands think the sun shines only for them."

Then, the captain of an Egyptian ship joined in.

"No, you are wrong," he said. "The sun is not a god, and it doesn't only move around India and its mountain. I have sailed across the Black Sea, the Arabian coast, and even as far as Madagascar and the Philippines. The sun shines on the entire world, not just India. It doesn't circle one mountain—it rises far to the east beyond Japan and sets far to the west beyond England. That's why the Japanese call their country 'Nippon,' which means 'the birthplace of the sun.' I know this because I have traveled to many places and have also heard stories from my grandfather, who sailed to the farthest parts of the ocean."

He was about to continue, but an English sailor in the group cut him off.

"No country understands the sun better than England," he said. "Everyone in England knows that the sun doesn't rise or set at all—it moves around the earth. We have proof of this because we just traveled around the world, and we never ran into the sun. No matter where we went, the sun showed up in the morning and disappeared at night, just like it does here."

The Englishman picked up a stick and started drawing circles in the sand, trying to explain how the sun moves through the sky. But he struggled to explain it clearly and finally pointed to the ship's pilot.

"This man knows more than I do," he said. "He can explain it better."

The pilot, who was a wise and well-traveled man, had been silently listening to the entire conversation. Now that everyone was watching him, he spoke.

"You are all confusing each other because you have been misled yourselves. The sun does not move around the earth—it is the earth that moves around the sun. As the earth spins, different parts of the world turn toward the sun every twenty-four hours. It's not just Japan, the Philippines, and Sumatra where we are now—the sun also shines on Africa, Europe, America, and many other places.

The sun does not exist just for one mountain, one island, or one sea. In fact, it doesn't even shine only for our planet—there are other worlds it reaches too. If you looked up at the sky instead of focusing only on the ground beneath your feet, you would understand this. Then you wouldn't believe that the sun exists just for you and your homeland."

The pilot spoke with certainty, having traveled far and studied the stars.

The Chinese scholar, a follower of Confucius, nodded and added,

"People make the same mistake about faith as they do about the sun. Pride leads them into arguments and confusion. Just as everyone wants the sun to shine only for them, each person wants a god who belongs only to them or their country. Every nation tries to fit the One who created everything into their own temples, even though the entire universe cannot contain Him.

But can anything made by human hands compare to the temple that God Himself has created to unite all people in truth and faith?"

"All human temples are built as copies of the greatest temple—God's world itself. Every temple has its water basins, high ceilings, lamps, statues or paintings, writings, sacred books, offerings, altars, and coffeehouse fell silent. No one argued anymore about whose faith was the greatest.

Thank You for Reading

Dear Reader,

We hope this timeless classic has sparked your imagination and enriched your literary journey. Now that you've turned the final page, we want to share a vision for the future of reading—one where every classic you've ever wanted to explore is at your fingertips, in a format that best suits your life.

We'd like to invite you to gain immediate, unlimited digital & audiobook access to hundreds of the most treasured literary classics ever written—along with the option to secure deluxe paperback, hardcover & box set editions at printing cost. Together, we can spark a new global literary renaissance alongside our small, independent publishing house called "The Library of Alexandria."

Thousands of years ago, the Library of Alexandria stood as a beacon of knowledge—until it was lost to history. We aim to reignite that spirit of preservation and discovery right now, in the modern age—only this time, it's accessible to all, in every language and every format.

Picture a world where every timeless classic, novel, poem, or philosophical treatise is not only available to read but also updated for today's readers—modernized, translated into any language or dialect, and ready to enjoy in any format you choose, whether that is in an eBook, audiobook, paperback, or deluxe hardcover & box set version a printing cost.

By joining our movement to rebuild the modern Library of Alexandria, you become part of an unprecedented mission to offer:

- **Unlimited Audiobook & eBook Access to the Greatest Classics of All Time**

  Instantly explore thousands of legendary works, from Plato and Shakespeare to Jane Austen and Leo Tolstoy. All are instantly ready to read or listen to, giving you a complete literary universe at your fingertips.

- **Paperback & Deluxe Editions at Printing Costs:**

  Purchase any title in a paperback, deluxe hardbound, or deluxe boxset edition at printing costs, shipped right to your doorstep. Curate your personal library of Alexandria with editions worthy of display—crafted to last, designed to captivate, and delivered straight to your door.

- **Modern translations for Contemporary Readers in all languages and dialects**

  Discover a vast selection of classics reimagined in clear, current language—no more struggling with outdated phrases or obscure references. Next to the original versions, we aim to offer translations in as many languages and dialects as possible.

  As we continue our translation efforts and add new languages, readers everywhere can connect with these works as if they were written today. By bridging linguistic divides, you're contributing to ensuring that these timeless stories become more meaningful, accessible, and inspiring for people across the globe.

- **Your Personal Library of Alexandria:**

  Over the months and years, you'll curate a unique physical archive of classics—each volume a testament to your taste, curiosity, and love of knowledge. It's not just about owning books—it's about curating a cultural legacy you'll cherish and pass down for generations to come.

- **Join a Global Literary Renaissance:**

  Your support fuels an ongoing mission: allowing us to reinvest in offering deluxe print editions (including special boxsets) at their true cost, broaden the range of available formats and translations, and extend the reach of these works to new audiences worldwide. By joining today, you're not just preserving a legacy of masterpieces; you set in motion a powerful wave of literary accessibility.

We are more than a publisher—we're a movement, and we can't do it alone. Your support lets us scale our mission, preserving and reimagining history's greatest works for tomorrow's readers.

Become a Torchbearer of knowledge.

Thank you for picking up this book and allowing us into your literary journey. As you turn the pages, know that you're part of something larger: a global effort to keep these stories alive, share their wisdom across borders and generations, and spark a true cultural revival for the modern era.

If this resonates with you—please consider taking the next step by visiting:

www.libraryofalexandria.com

With gratitude and a shared love of knowledge,

The Modern Library of Alexandria Team

Visit:

www.libraryofalexandria.com

Or scan the code below: